DEDICATION

To Children with Autism

And their families, teachers, and librarians who help them express their magic to the world.

— JD

To John and Rebecca —
For your support and inspiration.

— DH

Published by Citation Media LLC
91 Odyssey Drive
Chester, NY 10918

All rights reserved. No part of this book may be reproduced in any form
or by any electronic or mechanical means, including image storage
and retrieval systems, without permission in writing from the author,
except by a reviewer, who may quote brief passages in a review.
All illustrations used in this publication are used by license or permission
from the owner thereof, or are otherwise publicly available. All rights
and ownership regarding illustrations and characters featured in
Alex and His Magical Colors are the sole property of the author.

Printed in China

Author: Dr. Joe Denham
Illustrations: Denise Haley
Art Direction: Levitskie Creative

ISBN-10: 1-7341429-2-8
ISBN-13: 978-1-7341429-2-1
1C J21 1

Copyright 2021 by Dr. Joe Denham

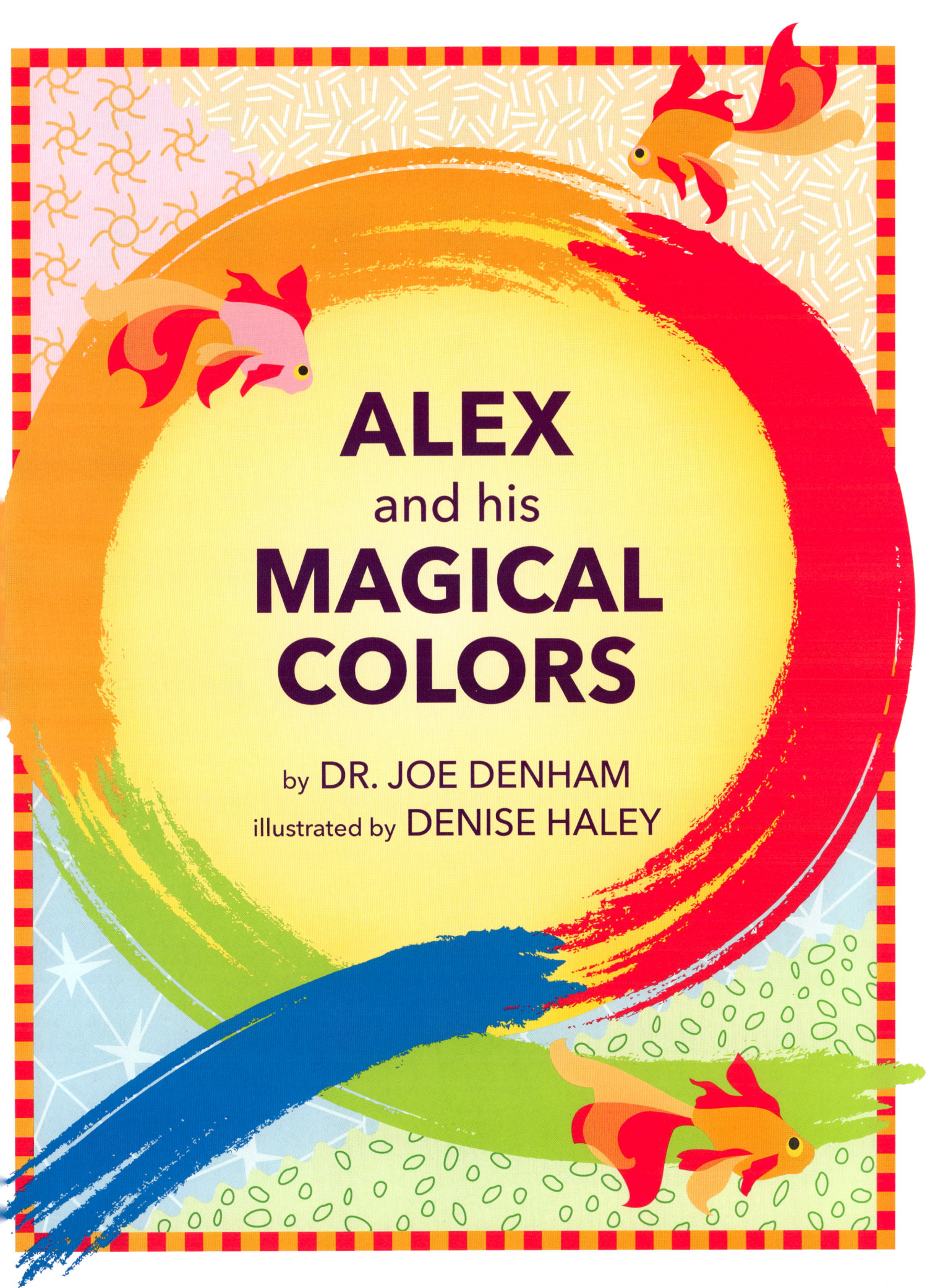

All the children laugh and scream as they run around playing baseball.

They cheer even louder when a girl hits a home run over the old, gray, gloomy wall.

But the children are sad when the game is over.

Because many old, gray, gloomy walls surround them in their neighborhood.

And Alex is sad too!

He wishes he could play with the children but his head hurts.

Alex wants to turn down
all the noise banging inside his head.

So he goes into his house.
He picks up his paint brush.
And starts to

paint...

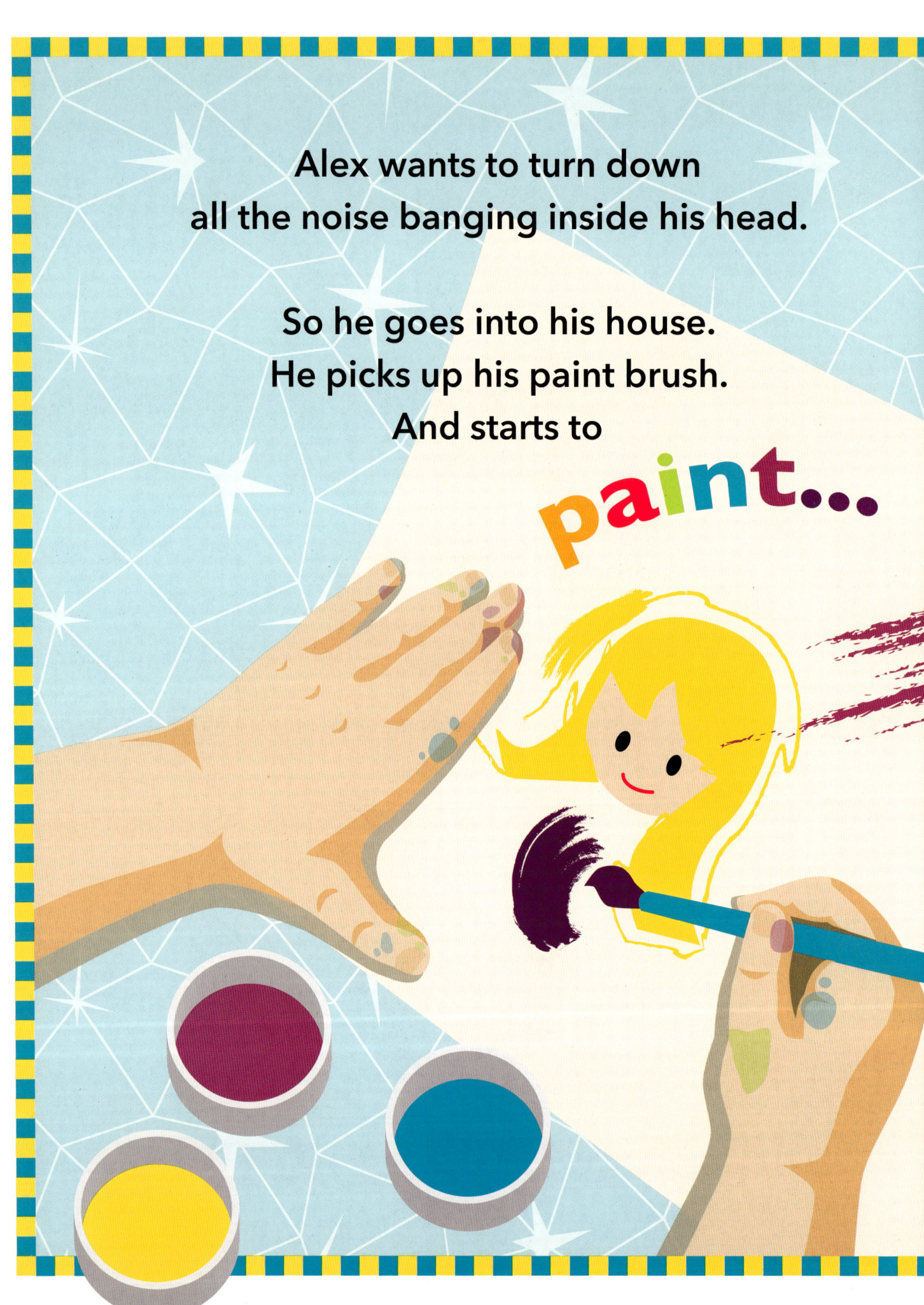

Alex paints pictures of…

His sister–

His puppy–

He even paints his cat and his goldfish.

Alex doesn't smile often.

But his paintings always make him feel happy!

Because there is no noise inside his head now.

Only colors twirling inside his head.

Then one day Alex and his Nana take a walk in the neighborhood.

Alex sees many sad people walking past these old, gray, gloomy walls.

Alex and Nana walk in the field.

"Nana, I wanted to play baseball with all the kids but I just couldn't," Alex said.

"What was wrong, Alex?" Nana said.

Then Alex stares at his hands.

And he stares at the old, gray, gloomy wall.

Suddenly he has a great idea!

Alex runs home and grabs
all the paint and brushes he can find.

Then he runs back to the old,
gray, gloomy wall.

Suddenly colors twirl across the wall!

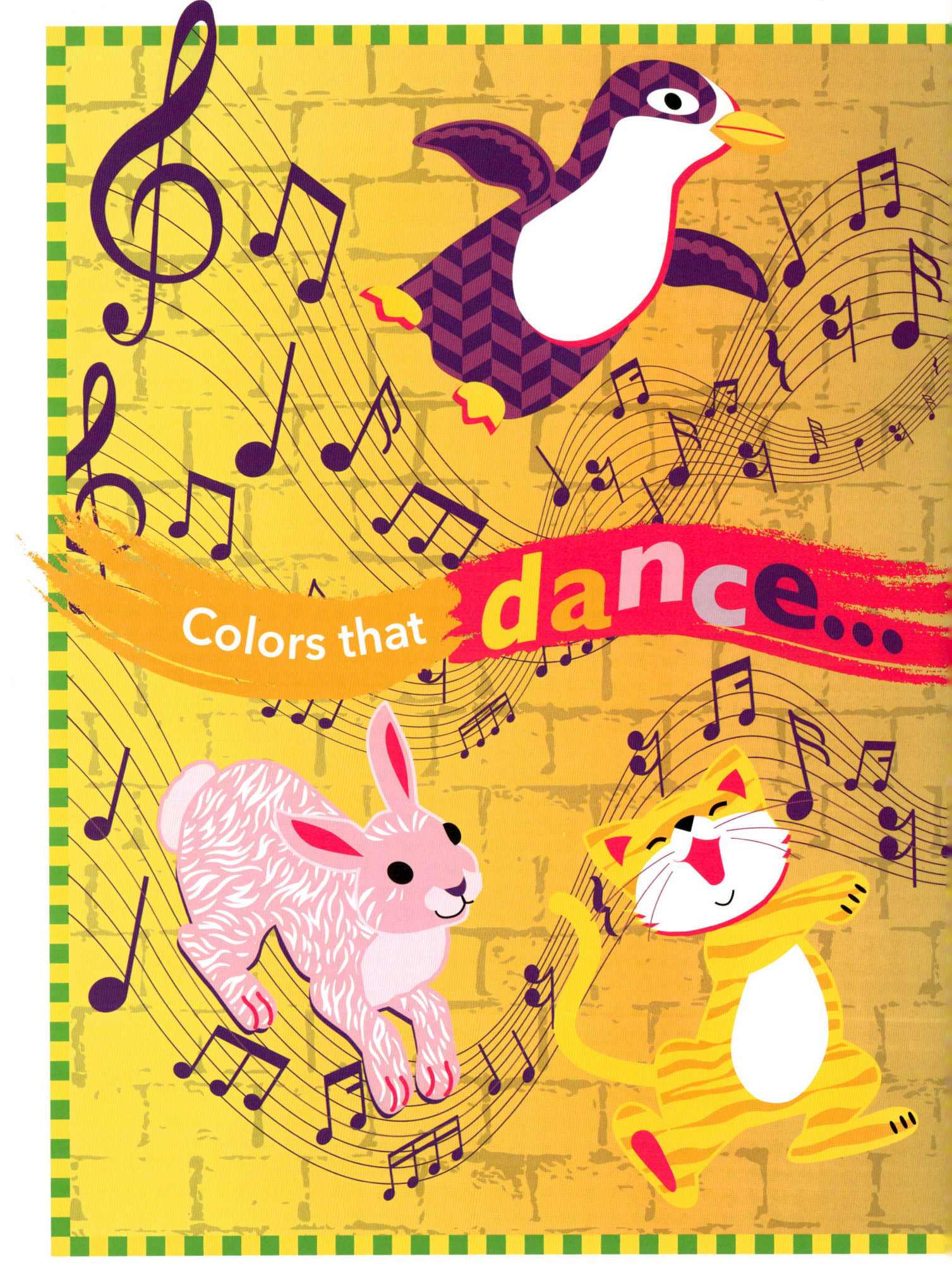

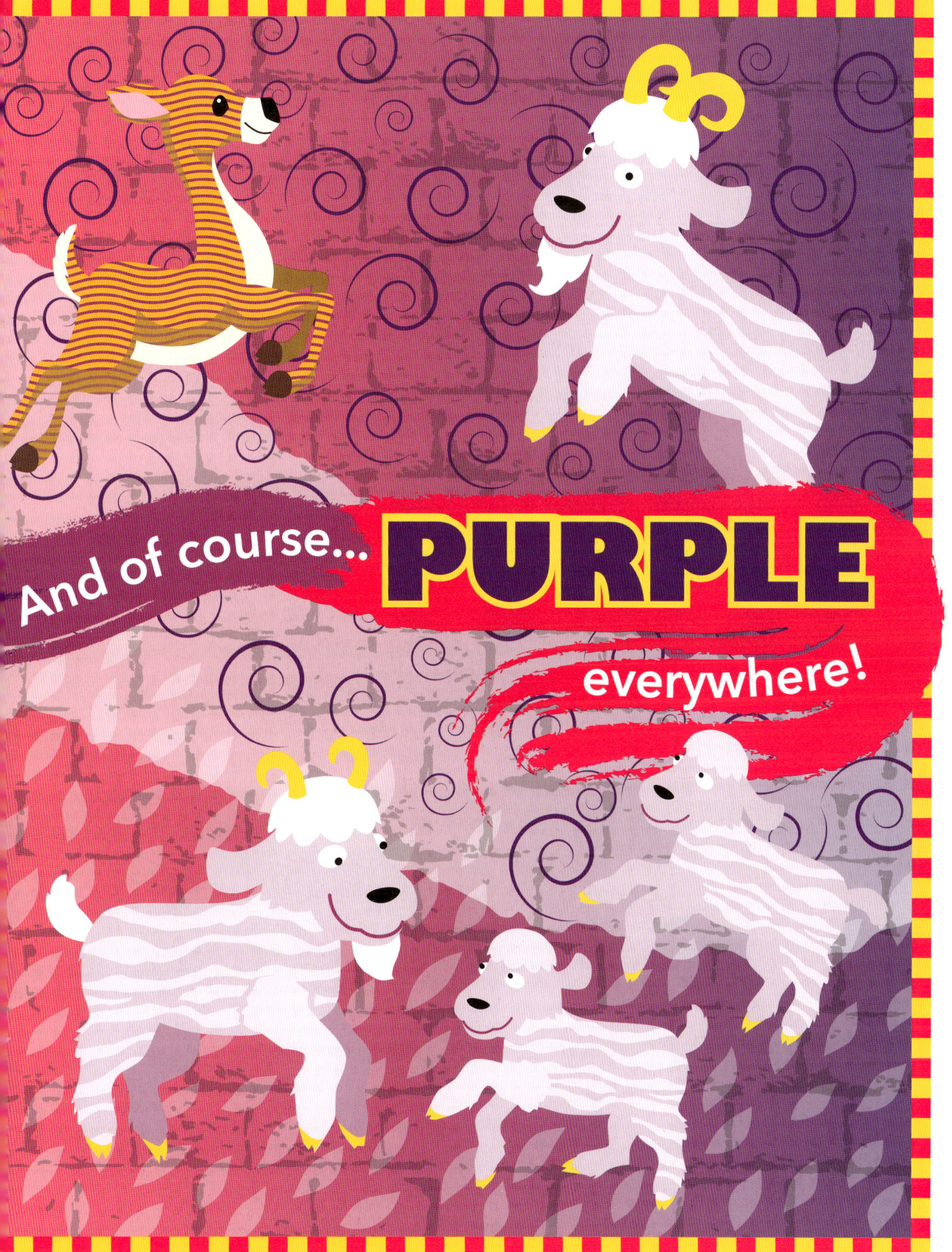

Everyone smiles as they watch Alex brush his magical colors across the wall.

But it is not an old, gray, gloomy wall anymore.

Now it is...
A beautiful wall of

ALEX'S MAGICAL COLORS!

"We're sorry loud noises hurt you. We'll always be here to help you, Alex," the children said.

Everyone asks Alex to paint more old, gray, gloomy walls with his magical colors.

"I would love to give you more paintings. But sometimes if I can't be outside, I am still here with you. Just look at my paintings!" Alex said.

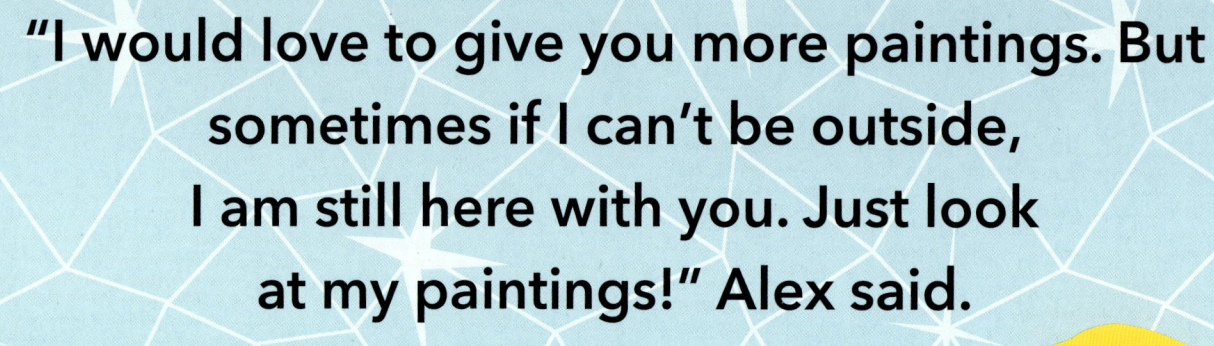

All of Alex's neighbors smile as they form a circle around their

Magical and Colorful Friend!

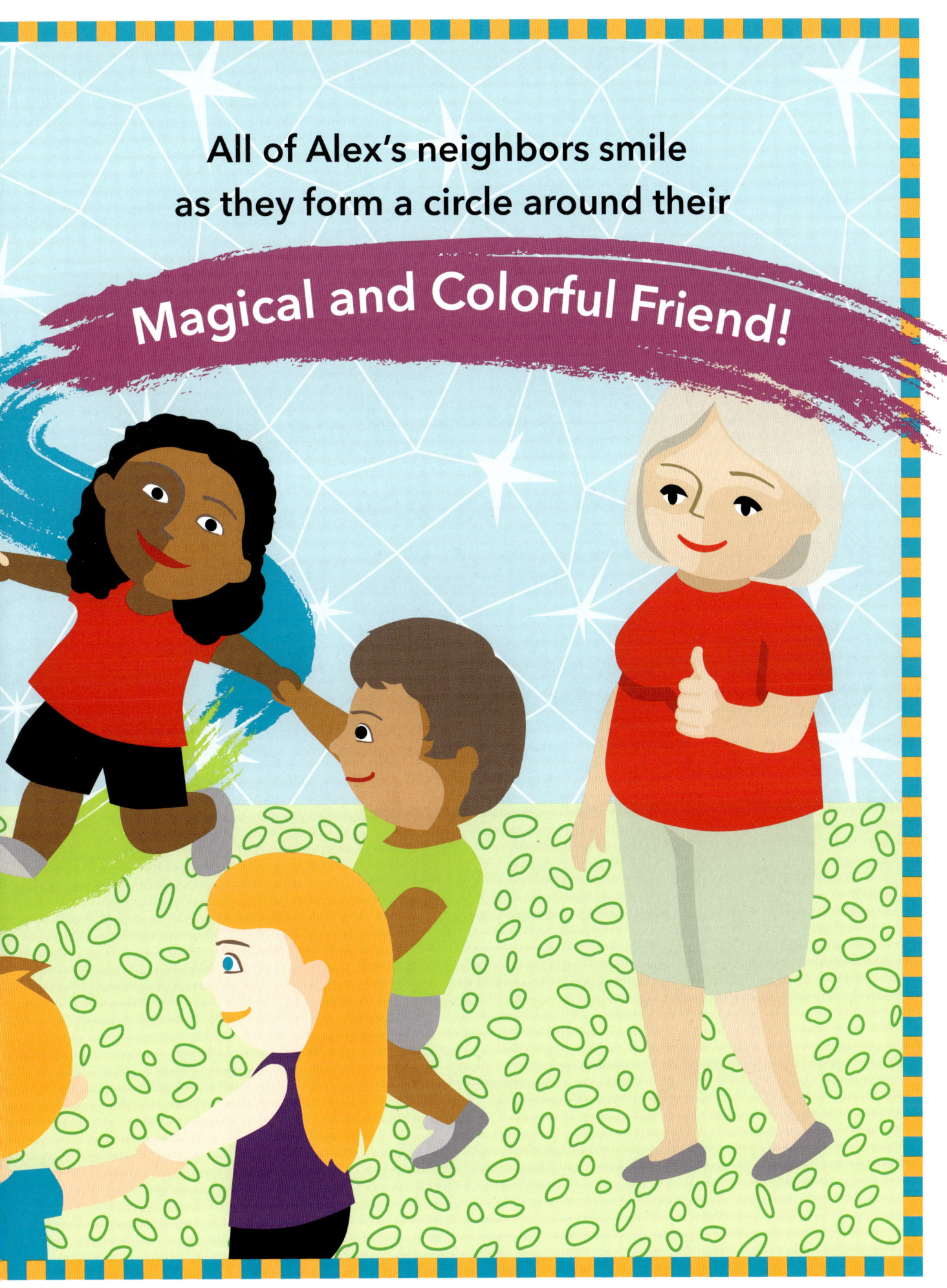

ALEX'S FUN ACTIVITIES

1. Your children can create their own Walls of Magical Colors.

   Using your children's favorite colors, paint colorful walls made of wood blocks or any type of canvas.

2. Ask your children why these favorite colors magically help them feel happy.

3. What pictures would your children like to paint on their walls?

4. Do loud noises or other things make your children's heads hurt, like Alex?

5. Alex creates his comfort zone when he paints his pictures.

   How do your children remove all the loud noise or other hurts from inside their heads?